The Garden Square

The Garden Square

Translated by Sonia Pitt-Rivers
and Irina Morduch

CALDER

CALDER PUBLICATIONS
an imprint of

ALMA BOOKS LTD
3 Castle Yard
Richmond
Surrey TW10 6TF
United Kingdom
www.calderpublications.com

The Garden Square first published in French in 1955
This translation first published by John Calder (Publishers) Limited in 1959
This revised edition first published by Calder Publications in 2018

© Éditions Gallimard, Paris, 1955, renewed in 1983
Translation © Calder Publications 1959, 2018

Cover design: Will Dady

Printed and bound by CPI Group (UK) Ltd, Croydon, CR0 4YY

ISBN: 978-0-7145-4850-0

The Garden Square

I

T HE CHILD CAME OVER QUIETLY from the far side of the square and stood beside the girl.

"I'm hungry," he announced.

The man took this as an opportunity to start a conversation.

"I suppose it is about teatime?"

The girl was not disconcerted: on the contrary, she turned and smiled at him.

"Yes, it must be nearly half-past four, when he usually has his tea."

She took two jam-covered bread slices from a basket beside her on the bench and handed them to the child, then skilfully knotted a bib around his neck.

"He's a nice child," said the man.

The girl shook her head as if in denial.

"He's not mine," she remarked.

The child moved off with his slices of bread. As it was a Thursday, the park was full of children: big ones playing with marbles or chasing each other, small ones playing in the sandpits, while smaller ones still sat patiently waiting in their prams for the time when they would join the others.

"Although," the girl continued, "he could be mine, and people often assume he is mine. But I have to tell them he's got nothing to do with me."

"I see," said the man. "I have no children either."

"Sometimes it seems strange, don't you think, that there should be so many children everywhere, and yet none of them are your own?"

"I suppose so, yes, when you come to think of it. But then, as you said, there are so many already."

"All the same…"

"But if you were fond of them, if they give you pleasure to watch, doesn't it matter less?"

"Couldn't the opposite also be true?"

"Probably. I expect it depends on one's nature: I think that some people are quite happy with the children who are already there, and I believe I am one of them. I have seen so many children and I could have had children of my own, and yet, you see, I manage to be quite satisfied with those of others."

"Have you really seen so many?"

"Yes. You see, I travel."

"I see," the girl said in a friendly manner.

"I travel all the time, except just now, of course, when I'm resting."

"Parks are good places to rest in, particularly at this time of year. I like them too. It's nice being out of doors."

"They cost nothing, they're always cheerful because of the children, and then if you don't know many people there's always the opportunity to start a conversation."

"That's true. Do you sell things when you travel?"

"Yes, that's my profession."

"Always the same things?"

"No, different things, but all of them small. You know those little things one always needs and so often forgets to buy. They all fit into a medium-sized suitcase. I suppose you could call me a travelling salesman, if you know what I mean."

"Like those people you see in markets selling things from an open suitcase?"

"That's right. I often work at the edges of street markets."

"I hope you don't think it rude of me to ask, but do you manage to make a living?"

"I've nothing to complain of."

"I thought that was probably the case."

"I don't mean to say that I earn a lot of money, but I earn a little something every day, and in its way I call that making a living."

"So you manage to make ends meet, if I may be so bold?"

"Yes, I think I just about make ends meet: I don't mean that every day is as good as the previous one. No. Sometimes things are a little tight, but in general I manage well enough."

"I'm glad."

"Thank you. Yes, I manage more or less and have really nothing to complain about. Being single with no home of my own, I have few worries, and the ones I have are naturally only for myself – sometimes for instance I find that I have run out of toothpaste, sometimes I might want for a little company. But on the whole it works out well. Thank you for asking."

"Would you say that almost anyone could do your work? As far as you can tell, I mean?"

"Yes indeed. I would even say that it is the best possible example of a job that can be done by everybody."

"You see, I should have thought it might need special skills?"

"Well I suppose it is better to know how to read, if only for the newspaper in the evenings at the hotel, and also of course for the names of the train stations. It makes life a little easier, but that's all. That's not much of a requirement and, you see, you can still make ends meet."

"I really meant other kinds of qualities: I would have thought your work needed endurance, or patience perhaps, and a great deal of perseverance?"

"I have never done any other work, so it's hard for me to tell. But I always imagined that the qualities you mention would be necessary for any work; in fact that there could hardly be a job where they are not needed."

"I am sorry to go on asking you all these questions, but do you think you will always go on travelling like this? Or do you think that one day you might stop?"

"I don't know."

"I'm sorry. Forgive me for being so curious, but we were talking…"

"It's quite all right. But I am afraid I don't know if I will go on travelling. There really is no other answer I can give you: I don't know. How does one know such things?"

"I only meant that if you travelled all the time, as you do, I would have thought that one day you would want to stop and stay in one place, that's all."

"It's true, I suppose, that one should want to stop. But how do you stop doing one thing and start another? How do people decide to leave one job for another, and why?"

"If I've understood correctly, the decision to stop travelling would depend only on yourself, not on anything else?"

"I don't think I have ever quite known how such things are decided. I have no particular attachments. In fact, I am a rather solitary person, and unless some great piece of luck came my way I cannot really see how I could change my work. And somehow I can't imagine where this luck would come from, from which part of my life. Of course I don't mean that it could not come my way one day – after all, one never knows – nor that if it did I would not accept it very gladly, but for the moment I must confess I cannot see much luck coming my way and helping me to a decision."

"But couldn't you just simply want it? I mean, couldn't you decide you wanted to change your work?"

"No, I don't think so. Every day I want to be clean, well fed and sleep well, and I also like to be decently dressed. So you see I hardly have time for wanting much more. And then, I must admit, I don't really dislike travelling."

"Can I ask you another question? How did all this start?"

"How could I begin to tell you? Stories like that are so long and so complicated, and sometimes I really think they are a little beyond me. It would mean going so far back that I feel tired before I start. But on the whole I think things happened to me as they do to anyone else, no differently."

A wind had risen, so light it seemed to hint at the approaching summer. For a moment it chased the clouds away, leaving a new warmth hanging over the city.

"How lovely it is," the man said.

"Yes," said the girl, "it's almost the beginning of the hot weather. From now on it will be a little warmer each day."

"You see, I had no special aptitude for any particular work or for any particular kind of life. And so I suppose I will go on as I am. Yes, I think I will."

"So really your feelings are only negative? They are just against any particular work or any particular life?"

"Against? No. That's too strong a word. I can only say that I have no very strong likes. I really just came to be as I am in the way that most people come to be as they are."

"But between the things that happened to you a long time ago and now, wasn't there time for you to change – almost every day in fact – and start liking things? Anything?"

"I suppose so. I don't deny it. For some people life must be like that, yes, and then again for others it is not. Some people must get used to the idea of never changing, and I think that really is true of me. So I expect I will just go on as I am."

"Well, for me things will not go on being the same."

"But can you know already?"

"Yes, I can, because my situation is not one which can continue: sooner or later it must come to an end. I am waiting to get married. And as soon as I am married, my present life will be quite finished."

"I understand."

"I mean that once it is over it will leave so few traces that it might as well never have been."

"Perhaps I too – after all, it's impossible to foresee everything, isn't it? – might change my life one day."

"Ah, but the difference is that I want to change mine. What I do now is hardly a job. People call it one to make things easier for themselves, but in fact it is not.

It's a state of being, a complete state of being, you understand, like for example being a child or ill. And so it must come to an end."

"I understand, but I've just come back from a long journey and now I'm resting. I never much like thinking of the future, and today, when I'm resting, even less: that's why I am so bad at explaining to you how it is I can put up with my life as it is and not change it, and not even be able to imagine changing. I'm sorry."

"Oh no, I'm the one who should apologize."

"Of course not. After all, we can always talk."

"That's right. And it has no consequences."

"And so you are waiting for something to happen?"

"Yes. I can see no reason why I should not get married one day like everybody else. As I told you."

"You're quite right. There is no reason at all why you should not get married too."

"Of course, in my current state – one which is so looked down upon – you could say that the opposite would be more true, and that there is no reason at all for it to happen. And so somehow I think that to make it seem quite ordinary and natural, I must want it with all my might. And that is how I want it."

"I am sure nothing is impossible. That's what people say, at least."

"I have thought about it a great deal: here I am, young, healthy and truthful, just like any woman you see anywhere whom some man has settled for. And surely it would be surprising if somewhere there isn't a man who won't see that I am just as good as anyone else and settle for me. I am full of hope."

"I am sure it will happen to you. But if you were suggesting that I make the same sort of change, I can only ask what I would do with a wife? I have nothing in the world but my suitcase, and I can barely sustain myself."

"Oh no, I did not mean to say that you need this particular change. I was talking of change in general. For me marriage is the only possible change, but for you it could be something else."

"I expect you are right, but you seem to forget that people are different. You see, however much I wanted to change, even if I wanted it with all my might, I could never manage to want it as much as you do. You seem to want it at all costs."

"Perhaps that is because for you a change would be less great than it would for me. As far as I am concerned, I feel I want the greatest change there could be. I might be mistaken, but it still seems to me that all the changes I see in other people are straightforward in comparison to the one I want for myself."

"But don't you think that even if everyone needed to change, and needed it very badly indeed, that even so they would feel differently about it according to their own particular circumstances?"

"I am sorry, but I must explain that I am quite uninterested in particular circumstances. As I told you, I am full of hope, and what is more I do everything possible to make my hopes come true. For instance every Saturday I go to the local dance hall and dance with anyone who asks me. They say that the truth will out, and I believe that one day someone will recognize in me a perfectly marriageable young woman, just as good as anyone else."

"I don't think it would help me to go dancing, you understand, even if I wanted a change, and a less radical one than yours. My profession is insignificant: in fact it can hardly even be called a profession, since it only just provides enough for one person, or perhaps it would be nearer the truth to say half a person. And so I couldn't, even for an instant, imagine that anything like that would change my life."

"But then perhaps, as I said before, it would be enough for you to change your work?"

"Yes, but how? How does one change a profession, even such a miserable one as mine? One which doesn't even allow me to marry? All I do is to go with my suitcase through one day to the next, from one night to another and even from one meal to the next meal, and there is no time for me to stop and think about it as perhaps I should. No, if I were to change, then the opportunity must come to me: I have no time to meet it halfway. And then again I should, perhaps, explain that I never felt that anyone particularly needed my services or my company – so much so that quite often I am amazed that I occupy any place in the world at all."

"Then perhaps the change you should make would be just to feel differently about things?"

"Of course. But you know how it is. After all, one is what one is, and how could anyone change so radically? Also, I have come to like my work, as paltry as it is: I like catching trains, and sleeping almost anywhere no longer bothers me much."

"You must not mind my saying this, but it seems to me that you should never have let yourself become like this."

"You could perhaps say I was always a little predisposed to it."

"For me it would be terrible to go through life with nothing for company but a suitcase full of things to sell. I think I should be frightened."

"Of course that can happen, especially at the beginning, but one gets used to little things like that."

"I think that in spite of everything I would rather be as I am, in my present position. But perhaps that is because I am only twenty."

"But you mustn't think that my work has nothing but disadvantages. That would be quite wrong. With all this time spent on the road, in trains, in squares like this, with all this time to think, you end up finding a way to justify leading one sort of existence over the other."

"But I thought you said you had only enough time to think of yourself? Or rather of supporting yourself financially and of nothing else?"

"No. What I lack is time to think of the future, but I have time to think of other things, or perhaps I should say I make it. Because if one can face struggling a little more than others do just to get enough to eat, it is only possible on condition that once a meal is over one can stop thinking about the whole problem. If immediately after finishing one meal you had to start thinking about the next one, it would be enough to drive you mad."

"I imagine so. But you see, what would drive me mad would be going from city to city as you do with no other company than a suitcase."

"Oh you're not always alone, you know. I mean so alone that you might go mad. No, there are boats and trains full of people to watch and listen to, and then, if you ever feel you are on the brink of going mad, there are always ways to avoid it."

"But what good would it do me to make the best of things, since all I want is to finish with my present position? In the end all your attitude does for you is to give you more reasons for not finishing with yours."

"That is not completely true, because should an opportunity arise for me to change my work I would certainly seize it; no, my attitude helps me in other ways. For example it helps me to see the advantages of my profession, such as travelling a great deal and of the feeling of becoming a little wiser than I was before. I am not saying I am right. I could easily be wrong and, without realizing it, have become far less wise than I ever was. But then, since I couldn't know, it doesn't really matter, does it?"

"And so you are continually travelling? As continually as I stay in one place?"

"Yes. And even if sometimes I go back to the same places, they can be different. In the spring, for instance, you will find cherries in the markets. That is what I really wanted to say, and not that I thought I was right in putting up with my life as it is."

"You're right. Quite soon, in two months, there will be cherries in the markets. I am glad for your sake. But tell me, what other things can you see on your travels?"

"Oh, a thousand things. One time it will be spring and another winter – either sunshine or snow, making the place unrecognizable. But I think it is really the cherries which change things the most: suddenly there they are, and the whole marketplace becomes scarlet. Yes, they will there in about two months. You see, that is what I wanted to explain – not that I thought my work was entirely satisfactory."

"But apart from the cherries in the markets and the sunshine and the snow, what else do you see?"

"Sometimes nothing much, nothing that you can see, even. But a number of little things added together seem to change a place. Places can be familiar and unfamiliar at the same time: a market which once seemed hostile can, quite suddenly, become warm and friendly."

"But isn't everything exactly the same sometimes?"

"Yes. Sometimes everything is so identical that it seems you left it only the night before. I have never understood how this could happen, because after all it would seem impossible that anything could remain so much the same."

"But apart from the cherries in the markets and the sunshine and the snow?"

"Well, sometimes a new block of flats which was half built when last I was there is finished and lived in: full of people and noise. And the odd thing is that although the town had never seemed overcrowded before, there it suddenly is – a brand-new block of flats, completed and inhabited as if it had always been utterly necessary."

"All the things you describe and the changes you notice are there for anyone to see, aren't they? They are not things which exist for you alone?"

"Sometimes there are things which I alone can see, but only negligible things. In general you are right: the things I notice are mostly changes in the weather, in buildings, things which anyone would notice. And yet sometimes, just by watching them carefully, such things can affect one just as much as events that are completely personal. In fact it feels as though they were personal, as if somehow I had put the cherries there myself."

"I see what you mean, and I am trying to put myself in your place, but it's no good: I still think I should be frightened."

"That does happen. It happens to me sometimes when I wake up at night, for example. But on the whole it is only at night that I feel frightened, although I can also feel it at dusk – but then only when it's raining or there's a fog."

"Isn't it strange that although I have never actually experienced the fear we are talking about, I can still understand a little what it must be like?"

"You see, it is not the kind of fear you might feel if you said to yourself that when you died no one would notice. No, it's another kind of fear, a general one which affects everything and not just you alone."

"As if you were suddenly terrified of being yourself, of being what you are instead of someone different, almost instead of being quite some other kind of thing, perhaps?"

"Yes. It comes from feeling at the same time like everyone else, exactly like everyone else, and yet being oneself. In fact I think it is just that: being one kind of thing rather than another..."

"It's complicated, but I understand."

"As for the other kind of fear – the fear of thinking that no one would notice if you died – it seems to me that sometimes this can make one happier. I think that if you knew that when you died no one would suffer, not even a small dog, it makes it easier to bear the thought of dying."

"I am trying to follow you, but I am afraid I don't understand. Perhaps because women are different from men? All I do know is that I could not bear to live as you do, alone with that suitcase. It is not that I would not like to travel, but unless there was someone who cared for me somewhere in the world I don't think I could do it. In fact I can only say that I would prefer to be where I am."

"But could you not think of travelling while waiting for what you want?"

"No. I don't believe you know what it is to want to change one's life. I must stay here and think about it, think with all my might, or else I know I will never manage to change."

"Perhaps, as you say, I don't really know."

"How could you know? Because however modest a way of life you have, it is at least yours. So how could you know what it is like to be nothing?"

"Am I right in thinking that no one would particularly care if you died either?"

"No one. And I've been twenty now for two weeks. But one day someone will care. I know it. I am full of hope. Otherwise nothing would be possible."

"You are quite right. Why shouldn't someone care about you as much as about anyone else?"

"That's just it. That's just what I say to myself."

"You're right, and now I'd like to ask you a question. Do you get enough to eat?"

"Yes thank you, I do. I eat as much as and even more than I need. Always alone, but you eat well in my job since, after all, you do the cooking – and good things too, even a leg of lamb sometimes. Not only do I have enough to eat, but I eat a great deal as well. I even have to force myself sometimes, because I feel I would like to be fatter and more impressive, so that people would notice me more. I think that if I were bigger and stronger I would stand a better chance of getting what I want. You may say I'm wrong, but it seems to me that if I were radiantly healthy people would find me more attractive. And so you see, we are really very different."

"Probably. But in my own way I also have a posi-tive attitude. I must have explained myself badly just now. I assure you that if I should ever want to change, why then I would set about it like everyone else."

"Sorry, but it is not very easy to believe you when you say that."

"Perhaps, but you see while I have nothing against hope in general, the fact is that there has never seemed much reason for it to concern me. And yet I feel that it would not take a great deal for me to feel that hope is as necessary to me as it is to others. It might only need the smallest bit of faith. Perhaps I lack the time for it, who knows? I don't mean the time I spend in trains thinking of this or that, or chatting with other people, no, I mean the other kind of time: the time anyone has, each day, to think of the one that follows. I just lack the time to start thinking about that particular subject and so discovering that it might mean something to me too."

"And yet it seems to me – forgive me again – as I think you yourself said, that there was a time when you were like everyone else, no?"

"Precisely, but almost so much so that I was never able to do anything about it. No one can be everything at once or, as you said, want everything at once, and personally I was never able to get over this difficulty. I could never make up my mind to choose a profession. But after all, I have travelled, my suitcase takes me to a great many places, and once I even went to a foreign country. I didn't sell much there, but I saw it. If anyone had told me some years ago that I should want to go there, I would never have believed them, and yet, you see, when I woke up one day I suddenly felt I would like to visit it and I went. Although very little has happened to me in my life, at least I managed that – I went to that country."

"But aren't there unhappy people in this country of yours?"

"Yes."

"And there are girls like me, waiting for something to happen?"

"I expect so, yes."

"So what is the point of it?"

"Of course it's true that people are unhappy and die there, and there are probably girls like you waiting hopefully for something to happen to them. But why not get to know that country instead of this one where we are, even if some things are the same? Why not see another country?"

"Because – and you may tell me that I am wrong – I am completely indifferent to it."

"Ah, but wait. There for instance the winters are less harsh than here: in fact you would hardly know it was winter…"

"But what use is a whole country to anyone, or a whole city or even the whole of one warm winter? It's no use: you can say what you like, but you can only be where you are when you are, and so what is the point?"

"But exactly. The town where I went ends in a big square surrounded by huge balustrades which seem to go on for ever."

"I am afraid I simply don't want to hear about it."

"The whole town is built in white limestone – imagine: it is like snow in the heart of summer. It is built on a peninsula surrounded by the sea."

"And the sea I suppose is blue. It is blue, isn't it?"

"Yes, it is blue."

"Well I am sorry, but I must tell you that people who talk of how blue the sea is make me sick."

"But how can I help it? From the zoo you can see it surrounding the whole town. And to anybody it must seem blue. It's not my fault."

"No. For me, without those ties of affection I was talking about, it would be black. And then, although I don't want to offend you in any way, you must see that I am much too preoccupied with my desire to change my life to be able to go away or travel or see new things. You can see as many towns as you like, but it never gets you anywhere. And once you have stopped looking, there you are, exactly where you were before."

"But I don't think we are talking about the same thing. I'm not talking of those huge events that change a whole life, no, just of the things which give pleasure while one is doing them. Travelling is a great distraction. Everyone has always travelled, the Greeks, the Phoenicians: it has always been so, all through history."

"It's true that we're talking of different things. To travel or see cities by the sea is not the kind of change I want. First of all I want to belong to myself, to own something, not necessarily something very wonderful, but something which is mine, a place of my own, maybe only one room, but mine. Why sometimes I even find myself dreaming of a gas stove."

"You know it would be just the same as travelling. You wouldn't be able to stop. Once you had the gas stove, you would want a refrigerator, and after that something else. It would be just like travelling, going from city to city. It would never end."

"Excuse me, but do you see anything wrong in my wanting something further perhaps after I have the refrigerator?"

"Of course not. No, certainly not. I was only speaking for myself, and as far as I am concerned I find your idea even more exhausting than travelling and then travelling some more, moving as I do from place to place."

"I was born and grew up like everyone else, and I know how to look around me: I look at things very carefully, and I can see no reason why I should remain as I am. I must start somehow, anyhow, to become of consequence. And if at this stage I began losing heart at the thought of a refrigerator I might never even possess the gas stove. And anyway, how am I to know if it would weary me or not? If you say it would, it might be because you have given the matter a great deal of thought, or perhaps even because at some time you got tired of one particular refrigerator."

"No, it is not that. Not only have I never possessed a refrigerator, but I have never had the slightest chance of doing so. No, it's only an idea, and if I talked of refrigerators like that it was probably only because to someone who travels they seem especially heavy and immobile. I don't suppose I would have made the same remarks about another object. And yet I do understand, I assure you, that it would be impossible for you to travel before you had the gas stove, or even, perhaps, the refrigerator. And I expect I am quite wrong to be so easily discouraged at the mere thought of a refrigerator."

"Yes, it does seem very strange."

"There was one day in my life, just one, when I no longer wanted to live. I was hungry, and as I had no money it was absolutely essential for me to work if I was to eat. It was as if I had forgotten that this was as true of everyone as of me! That day I felt quite unused to life, and there seemed no point in going on living, because I couldn't see why things should go on for me as they did for other people. It took me a whole day to get over this feeling. Then, of course, I took my suitcase to the market, and afterwards I had a meal and things went on as they had before, but with this difference – that ever since that day I find that any thought of the future, and after all thinking of a refrigerator is thinking of the future, is much more frightening than before."

"I would have guessed that."

"Since then, when I think about myself, it is simply in terms of one person more or one less, and so you see that a refrigerator more or less can hardly seem as important to me as it does to you."

"Tell me, did this happen before or after you went to that country you liked so much?

"After. But when I think about that country I feel pleased, and I think it would have been a pity for one more person not to have seen it. I don't mean that I imagine I was especially made to appreciate it. No, it just seems to me that since we are here, it is better to see one country more rather than one less."

"I can't feel as you do, and yet I do understand what you are saying, and I think you are right to say it. What you really mean is that since we are alive anyhow it is better to see things than not to see them, is it not? It was that you meant, wasn't it? And that seeing them makes the time pass quickly and more pleasantly?"

"Yes, it is a little like that. Perhaps the only difference between us is that we feel differently about how to spend or not spend our time?"

"Not only that, because as yet I have not had the time to become tired of anything, except of waiting of course. Don't misunderstand me: I don't mean that you are necessarily happier than I am, but simply that

if you were unhappy you could imagine something
which would help, like moving to another city, selling
something different, or even... even bigger things. But
I can't start thinking of anything yet, not even the
smallest thing. Nothing has begun for me except, of
course, for the fact that I am alive. There are times, in
summer for example when the weather is fine, when
I feel that something might have begun for me even
without there being any proof of it, and then I am
frightened. I become frightened of giving in to the
fine weather and forgetting what I want even for a
second, of losing myself in something unimportant,
of forgetting the most important thing. I am sure that
if at this stage I started thinking of details, I would
be lost."

"But it seemed to me for instance that you were fond
of that little boy?"

"It makes no difference. If I am, I don't want to
know it. If I started finding consolations in my life, if
I were able, to however small a degree, to put up with
it, then, again, I know I would be lost. I have a great
deal of work to do, and I do it. Indeed I am so good
at my work that each day they give me a little more
to do, and I accept it. Naturally it has ended in them
giving me the hardest things to do, dreadful things,

and yet I do them and I never complain. Because if I refused it would mean that I imagined that my situation, as it stands, could be improved, become milder, that it could be made somehow more bearable – and then, of course, it would end up one day by becoming bearable, full stop."

"And yet it seems strange to be able to make one's life easier and refuse to do so."

"I suppose so, but I never refuse to do anything, have never refused to do whatever is asked of me. I have never refused anything, although it would have been easy at the beginning, and now it would be easier still since I am asked to do more and more. But for as long as I can remember it has always been like this: I accepted everything quite quietly, so that one day I would be quite unable to accept anything any more. You may say that this is a rather childish way of looking at things, but I could never find another way of being sure that I would get what I wanted. You see, I know that people can get used to anything, and all around me I see people who are still where I am, but ten years later. There is nothing people cannot get accustomed to, even to a life like mine, and so I must be careful, very careful indeed, not to become accustomed to it myself. Sometimes

I am frightened, yes, because although I am aware of this danger, it is still so great that I am afraid that even I, aware as I am, might give in to it. But please go on telling me about the changes you see when you travel, apart from the snow, the cherries and the new buildings?"

"Well, sometimes the hotel has changed hands and the new owner is friendly and talkative where the old one was tired of trying to please and never spoke to his clients."

"Tell me, it is true, isn't it, that I must not take things for granted: that each day I must still be amazed to be where I am or else I shall never succeed?"

"I think that everyone is amazed, each day, to be still where they are. I think people are amazed quite naturally. I doubt if one can decide to be amazed at one thing more than at another."

"Each morning I am a little more surprised to find myself still where I am. I don't do it on purpose: I just wake up and, immediately, I am surprised. Then I start remembering things... I was a child like any other: there was nothing to show I was different. At cherry time, for instance, we used to go and steal fruit in the orchards. We were stealing it right up to the last day, because it was in that season that I was sent into service. But tell me more about the things you see when you travel, apart from what you have already told me, including the hotel owner?"

"I used to steal cherries like you, and there was nothing which seemed to make me different from other children, except perhaps that even then I loved them very much. Well, apart from a new hotel owner, sometimes a new wireless has been installed. That's a big change, when a café without music suddenly becomes a café with music: then of course they have many more customers and everyone stays much later. And that makes one more enjoyable evening to the good."

"You said to the good?"

"Yes."

"Ah, I sometimes think if only we had known… My mother simply came up to me and said, 'Come along now, it's over, come, it's over.' And I just let myself be led away like an animal to the slaughterhouse. Ah! If only I had known then, I promise you I would have fought. I would have saved myself. I would have begged my mother to let me stay. I would have persuaded her, oh how I would have!"

"But we didn't know."

CHAPTER I

"The cherry season went on that year like all the others. People would pass under my window singing, and I would be there behind the curtains watching them, and I got scolded for it."

"I was left free to pick cherries for a long time."

"There was I behind the window like a criminal, and yet my only crime was to be sixteen. But you? You said you went on picking them for a long time?"

"Longer than most people. And yet you see..."

"Tell me more about your cafés full of people and music."

"I don't really think I could go on living without them. I like them very much."

"I think I would like them too. I can see myself at the bar with my husband, listening to the wireless. People would talk to us and we would make conversation. We would be with each other and with the others. Sometimes I feel how nice it would be to go and sit in a café, but if you are a single young woman you can hardly afford to do so."

"I forgot to add that sometimes someone looks at you."

"I see, and comes over?"

"Yes, they come over."

"For no reason?"

35

"For no particular reason, but then the conversation somehow becomes less general."

"And then?"

"I never stay longer than two days in any town. Three at the most. The things I sell are not so essential."

"Alas."

The wind, which had died down, rose again, scattering the clouds, and once more the sudden warmth in the air brought thoughts of approaching summer.

"But the weather is really wonderful today," the man said again.

"It is nearly summer."

"Perhaps the truth is that one never really starts anything: perhaps things are always in the future?"

"If you can say that, it is because each day is full enough to prevent you thinking of the next. But for me the present is empty, a desert."

"But don't you ever do anything of which you could say later you had at least achieved something?"

"No, nothing. I work all day, but I never do anything of which I could say what you have just said. I cannot even think in those terms."

"Again, please don't think I want to contradict you, but you must see that whatever you do, this time you are living now will count for you one day.

You will look back on this desert as you describe it and discover, with startling precision, that it was not empty at all, but full of people. You won't be able to escape it. We think nothing has started and yet it has. We think we are doing nothing, but all the time we are doing something. We think we are going towards some solution, and then we pause and turn around, and there the solution is, behind us. It was like that with that city: at the time I did not appreciate it for what it was. The hotel was indifferent, they had let the room I had reserved, it was late and I was hungry. Nothing was waiting for me in that city except the city itself, vast – and try and imagine what a vast city, utterly absorbed in its own occupations, can be like for a tired traveller seeing it for the first time."

"I cannot imagine it."

"Nothing is waiting for you except a nasty room giving onto a noisy, dirty courtyard. And yet, looking back on it, I know that that voyage changed me, that much of what I had seen and done before led up to it and so became clear and understandable. It is only afterwards that we know whether we have been in such or such a city; you should be aware of that."

"If you mean things in that sense, perhaps you are right. Perhaps things have begun for me, and that they began on that particular day when I wanted them to."

"Yes, you see we think nothing happens, and yet, in your case, it seems to me that perhaps the most important thing that will have happened in your life is just this decision you have made not to begin living yet."

"I understand you, I really do, but you must also try and understand me. Even if that moment is past, I can't know it as yet, and I haven't the time to understand it. I hope one day I will know, as you did with your journey, and that when I look back everything behind me will be clear and fall into place. But now, at this moment, I am too involved to be able even to guess at what I might feel one day."

"Yes. And I know that probably it is impossible to make you understand things you have not yet felt, but all the same it is hard for me not to try and explain them to you."

"You are very kind, but I am afraid that I am not very good yet at understanding the things I am told."

"Believe me that I do understand all you have said, but even so, is it absolutely necessary to do all that work? Of course I am not trying to give you any advice, but don't you think that someone else would make a little effort and still manage, without quite so much work, to have as much hope for the future as before? Don't you think that another person would manage that?"

"Are you frightened that one day, if I have to wait too long and go on working a little more each day without complaining, I might suddenly lose patience altogether?"

"I admit that the kind of willpower you possess is a little frightening, but that's not why I made my suggestion. It was just because it is difficult to accept that someone of your age should live as you *do*."

"But I have no alternative. I have thought about it a great deal, I assure you."

"May I ask you how many people you work for?"

"Seven."

"And how many storeys?"

"Six."

"And rooms?"

"Eight."

"It's too much."

"But no. That's not the way to think. I must have explained myself very badly, because you haven't understood."

"I think that work can always be measured, and that, no matter what the circumstances, work is always work."

"Not my kind. One could say of that kind of work that it is better to do too much than too little. If there was time over to think or start enjoying oneself then one would really be lost."

"And you're only twenty."

"Yes, and, as they say, I've not yet had time to do any wrong. But that seems beside the point to me."

"On the contrary, I have a feeling that it is not, and that the people you work for should remember it."

"After all, it's hardly their fault if I agree to do all the work they give me. I would do the same in their place."

"I should like to tell you how I went into that town, after leaving my suitcase at the hotel."

"Yes I should like to hear that. But you mustn't worry on my account: I would be most surprised if I let myself become impatient. I think all the time of the risk I would run if that should happen, and so, you see, I don't think it will."

"It was only in the evening, after leaving my suitcase…"

"You see people like me do think too. There is nothing else for us to do, buried in our work. We think a great deal, but not like you. We have dark thoughts, and all the time."

"It was evening, just before dinner, after work."

"People like me think of the same things, of the same people, and our thoughts are always bad. That's why we are so careful and why it's not worth bothering about us. You were talking of jobs, and I wonder if something could be called a job which makes you spend your whole day thinking ill of people? But you were saying it was evening, and you had left your suitcase?"

"Yes. It was only towards the evening, after I had left my suitcase at the hotel, just before dinner, that I started walking through that town. I was looking for a restaurant, and of course it's not always easy to find exactly what one wants when price is a consideration. And while I was looking, I strayed away from the centre and came by accident to the zoo. A wind had risen. People had forgotten the day's work and were strolling through the gardens, which, as I've told you, were up on a hill overlooking the town."

"But I know that life is good. Otherwise, why on earth should I take so much trouble?"

"I don't really know what happened. The moment I entered those gardens I became a man utterly fulfilled by life."

"How could a garden, just seeing a garden, make a man happy?"

"And yet what I am telling you is quite an ordinary experience, and other people will often tell you similar things in the course of your life. I am a person for whom talking, for example, is a blessing, and suddenly in these gardens I was so completely at home, so much at my ease, that it might have been made especially for me as much as for the others. I don't know how to put it any better, except perhaps to say that it was as if I had achieved something and become, for the first time, equal to my life. I could not bear to leave the gardens. The wind had risen, the light was honey-coloured and even the lions whose manes glowed in the setting sun were yawning with the pure pleasure of being there. The air smelt of lions and of fire, and I breathed it as if it were the essence of friendliness which had, at last, included me. All the passers-by were preoccupied with each other, basking in the evening light. I remember thinking they were like the lions. And suddenly I was happy."

"But in what way were you happy? Like someone resting? Like someone who is cool again after having been very hot? Or happy as other people are happy every day?"

"More than that I think. Probably because I was unused to happiness. A great surge of feeling over-whelmed me, and I did not know what to do with it."

"A feeling which hurt?"

"Perhaps, yes. It hurt because there seemed to be nothing which could ever appease it."

"But that, I think, is hope."

"Yes that is hope, I know that really is hope. And of what? Of nothing. Just the hope of hope."

"You know, if there were only people like you in the world, no one would get anywhere."

"But listen. You could see the sea from the bottom of each avenue in that garden, every single one led to the sea. Actually the sea usually plays very little part in my life, but in those gardens they were all looking at the sea, even the people who were born there – even, it seemed to me, the lions themselves. How can you avoid looking at what other people are looking at, even if normally it doesn't mean much to you?"

"The sea couldn't have been as blue as all that, since you said the sun was setting?"

"When I left my hotel it was blue, but after I had been in those gardens a little while it became darker and calmer."

"But you said a wind had come up: it couldn't have been as calm as all that?"

"But it was such a gentle wind, if you only knew, and it was probably only blowing on the heights: on the town and not on the plain. I don't remember exactly from which direction it came, but surely not from the open sea."

"And then again, the setting sun couldn't have illuminated all the lions. Not unless all the cages faced the same way on the same side of the gardens looking towards the setting sun?"

"And yet I promise you it was like that. They were all in the same place and the setting sun lit up each lion without exception."

"And so the sun did set first over the sea?"

"Yes, you're quite right. The city and the garden were still in sunshine, while the sea was already in shade. That was three years ago. That's why I remember it all so well and like talking about it."

"I understand. One thinks one can get by without talking, but it's not possible. From time to time I find myself talking to strangers too, in this very garden square, just as we are talking now."

"When people need to talk it can be felt very strongly, and strangely enough people in general seem to resent it. It is only in squares that it seems quite natural. Tell me again, you said there were eight rooms where you worked? Big rooms?"

"I couldn't really say, since I don't suppose anyone else would see them in quite the same way as I do. Most of the time they seem big, but perhaps they're not as big as all that. It really depends on the day. On some days they seem endless and on others they seem so tiny that I think I could suffocate. But why did you ask?"

"It was only out of curiosity. For no other reason."

"I know that I must seem stupid to you, but I can't help it."

"I would say you are a very ambitious person, if I have really understood you, someone who wants everything that everyone else has, but wants it so much that one could almost be lead to thinking… one could almost find this desire… heroic."

"That word doesn't frighten me, although I had not thought of it in that way. You could almost say I have so little that I could have anything. After all, I could want to die with the same violence as I want to live. And is there anything, any one little thing in my life to which I could sacrifice my courage? And who or what could weaken it? Anyone would do the same as I do: anyone, I mean, who wanted what I want as much as I do."

"I expect so. Since everyone does what he thinks he has to do. Yes, I expect there are cases where it is impossible to be anything else but heroic."

"You see, if just once I refused the work they give me, no matter what it was, it would mean that I had begun to manage things, to defend myself, to take an interest in what I was doing. It would start with one thing, go on to another and could end anywhere. I would begin to defend my rights so well that I would take them seriously and end by thinking they existed. They would matter to me. I wouldn't be bored any more, and so I would be lost."

There was a silence between them. The sun, which had been hidden by the clouds, came out again. Then the girl started talking once more.

"Did you stay on in that town after being so happy in those gardens?"

"I stayed for several days. This can happen."

"Tell me, do you think that this can happen to everyone?"

"There must be some people to whom it has never happened. It's an almost unbearable idea, but I suppose there are such people."

"You don't know for certain do you?"

"No. I can easily be mistaken. The fact is I really don't know."

"And yet you seem to know about these things."

"No more than anyone else."

"There's something else I want to ask you: as the sun sets very quickly in those countries, surely, even if it set first on the sea, the shade must have reached the town soon afterwards, right? The sunset must have been over very soon, perhaps ten minutes after it had begun."

"You are quite right, and yet I assure you it was just at that moment that I arrived: just at the moment when everything is alight."

"Oh, I believe you."

"It doesn't sound as though you do."

"But I do, completely. And, anyway, you could have arrived at any other moment, without changing all that followed, couldn't you?"

"Yes, but I did arrive then, even if that moment only lasts for a few minutes a day."

"But that isn't really the point, is it?"

"No, that isn't really the point."

"And afterwards?"

"Afterwards the gardens were the same, except that it became night. A coolness came up from the sea and people were happy, for the day had been hot."

"But even so, eventually you had to eat?"

"Suddenly I was no longer very hungry. I was thirsty. I didn't have dinner that evening. Perhaps I just forgot about it."

"But that's why you had left your hotel – to eat, I mean?"

"Yes, but then I forgot about it."

"For me, you see, the days are like the night."

"But that is because you want them to be like that, isn't it? You would like to emerge from your present situation just as you were when you entered it, as one wakes up from a long sleep. I know, of course, what it is to want to create night all around one, but, you see, it seems to me that however hard one tries the dangers of the day break through."

"Only my night is not as dark as all that, and I doubt if the day is really a threat to it. I'm twenty. Nothing has happened to me yet. I sleep well. But one day I must wake up once and for all. It must happen."

"And so each day passes by in the same way for you, even though they may be different?"

"Tonight, like every Thursday night, there will be people for dinner. I will eat lamb all alone in the kitchen at the end of the corridor."

"And the murmur of their conversation will reach you the same way, so very much the same that you could imagine that each Thursday they said exactly the same things?"

"Yes, and as usual I won't understand anything they talk about."

"And you will be all alone, there in the kitchen, surrounded by the remnants of the leg of lamb in a sort of drowsy lull. And then you will be called to take away the meat plates and serve the next course."

"They will ring for me, but they won't waken me. I serve at table half-asleep."

"Just as they are waited on, in absolute ignorance of what you might be like. And so in a way you are quits: they can neither make you happy nor sad, and so you sleep."

"Yes. And then the guests will leave and the house will be quiet till the morning."

"When you will start ignoring them all over again, while trying to wait on them as well as possible."

"I expect so. But I sleep well! If you only knew how well I sleep. There is nothing they can do to disturb my sleep. But why are we talking about these things?"

"I don't know, perhaps just to make you remember them."

"Perhaps it is that. But you see one day, yes one day, at the time it will be two hours and a half from now, I shall go into the drawing room and I shall speak."

"Yes, you must."

"I shall say: 'This evening I shall not be serving dinner.' Madam will turn round in surprise. And I will say: 'Why should I serve dinner since, as from this evening… as from this evening…' but no, I cannot even imagine how things of such importance are said."

The man made no reply. He seemed only attentive to the softness of the wind, which once more had risen. The girl seemed to expect no response to what she had just said.

"Soon it will be summer," said the man and added with a groan, "We really are the lowest of the low."

"Why us rather than others?"

"They say that someone has to be."

"Yes, indeed, and that everything has its place."

"And yet sometimes one wonders why this should be so."

"Yes. Although sometimes, in cases like ours, one wonders whether being us or someone else makes any difference. Sometimes one just wonders."

"Yes, and sometimes, in certain instances, that is ultimately a consoling thought."

"Not for me. That could never be a consoling thought. I must believe that I myself am concerned rather than anyone else. Without that belief I am lost."

"Who knows? Perhaps things will soon change for you, soon and very suddenly. Perhaps even this very summer you will go into that drawing room and announce that, as from that moment, the world can manage without your services."

"Who knows indeed? And you could call it pride, but when I say the world, I really mean the whole world. Do you understand?"

"Yes I do."

"I will open the door of that drawing room and then, suddenly, everything will be said once and for all."

"And you will always remember that moment as I remember my journey. I have never been on so wonderful a journey since, nor one which made me so happy."

"Why are you suddenly so sad? Do you see anything sad in the fact that one day I must open that door? On the contrary, doesn't it seem the most desirable thing in the world?"

"It seems utterly desirable to me, and even more than that. No, if I felt a little sad when you talked of it – and I did feel a little sad – it was only because once you have opened that door it will have been opened for ever, and afterwards you will never be able to do it again. And then, sometimes, it seems so hard, so very hard to go back to a country which pleased me as well as that one that I told you about, that occasionally I wonder if it would not have been better never to have seen it at all."

"I'm sorry, but you must see I cannot understand what it is like to have seen that city and to want to go back to it, nor can I understand the sadness you seem to feel at the thought of waiting for that moment. You could try as hard as you liked to tell me there was something sad about it, I could never understand. I know nothing, or rather I know nothing except this: that one day I must open that door and speak to those people."

"Of course, of course. You mustn't take any notice of what I say. Those thoughts simply came into my mind when you were talking, but I didn't want them to discourage you. In fact quite the opposite: I'd like to ask you more about that door. What special moment are you waiting for to open it? For instance, why couldn't you do it this evening?"

"I could never do it alone."

"You mean that being without money or education you could only begin in the same way all over again and that really there would be no point to it?"

"I mean that and other things. I don't really know how to describe it, but being alone I feel as if I had no meaning. I can't change by myself. No. I will go on visiting that dance hall, and one day a man will ask me to be his wife. Then I will open that door. I couldn't do it before that happened."

"How do you know if it would turn out like that if you have never tried?"

"I have tried. And because of that I know that alone... outside of this position, perhaps, all alone in a city... I would be, as I said, somehow meaningless. I wouldn't know what I wanted any more, perhaps wouldn't even know who I was exactly, wouldn't know what it was to want to change. I would simply be there, doing nothing, telling myself that nothing was worthwhile."

"I think I see what you mean: in fact I believe I understand it all."

"One day someone must choose me. Then I will be able to change. I don't mean this is true for everyone. I am simply saying it is true for me. I have already tried and I know. I don't know all this just because I know what it is like to be hungry, no, but because when I was hungry I realized I didn't care. I hardly knew who it was in me who was hungry."

"I understand all that: I can see how one could feel like that... in fact I can guess it, although personally I have never felt the need to be singled out as you want to be – or perhaps I really mean that if such a thought ever did cross my mind I never attached much importance to it."

"You must understand, you must try to understand that I have never been wanted by anyone, ever, except of course for my capacity for housework, and that is not choosing me as a person but simply wanting something impersonal which makes me as anonymous as possible. And so I must be wanted by someone, just once, and even if only once. Otherwise I shall exist so little even to myself that I would be incapable of knowing how to want to choose anything. That is why, you see, I attach so much importance to marriage."

"Yes, I do see, but in spite of all that, and with the best will in the world, I cannot really see how you hope to be chosen when you cannot make a choice for yourself?"

"I know it seems ridiculous, but that is how it is. Because you see, left to myself, I would find any man suitable: any man in the world would seem suitable on the one condition that he wanted me just a little. A man who so much as noticed me would seem desirable just for that very reason, and so how on earth would I be capable of knowing who would suit me when anyone would, on the one condition that they wanted me? No, someone else must decide for me, must guess what would be best. Alone I could never know."

"Even a child knows what is best for him."

"But I am not a child, and if I let myself go and behaved like a child and gave in to the first temptation I came across – after all, I am perfectly aware that it is there at every street corner – why then I would follow the first person who came along, the first man who just wanted me. And I would follow him simply for the pleasure I would have in being with him, and then, why then I would be lost, completely lost. You could say that I could easily make another kind of life for myself, but as you can see I no longer have the courage even to think of it."

"But have you never thought that if you leave this choice entirely to another person it need not necessarily be the right one and might make for unhappiness later?"

"Yes, I have thought of that a little, but I cannot think now, before my life has really begun, of the harm I might possibly do later on. I just say one thing to myself and that is, if the very fact of being alive means that we can do harm, however much we don't want to, just by choosing or making mistakes, if that is an inevitable state of affairs, why then, I too will go through with it. If I have to, if everyone has to, I can live with harm."

"Please don't get so excited: there will be someone one day who will discover that you exist both for him and for others – you must be sure of that. And yet you know one can almost manage to live with this lack of which you speak."

"Which lack? Of never being chosen?"

"If you like, yes. As far as I am concerned, I should be so surprised if anyone chose me, that I should simply laugh, I believe, if it actually happened in the end."

"While I should be in no way surprised. I am afraid I would find it perfectly natural. It is just the contrary – the fact that no one has chosen my yet – which aston-ishes me, and it astonishes me more each day. I cannot understand it, and I never get used to it."

"It will happen. I promise you."

"Thank you for saying so. But are you saying that just to please be, or can people tell these things? Can you guess it already just from talking to me?"

"I expect such things can be guessed, yes. To tell you the truth, I said that without thinking much, but not at all because I thought it would please you. It must have been because I could see it."

"And you? How are you so sure the opposite is true of you?"

"Well, I suppose it is because... Yes, just because I am not surprised. I think it must be that. I am not at all surprised that no one has chosen me, while you are so amazed that you have not yet been singled out in the way that you want."

"In your place, you know, I would force myself to want something, however hard it might be. I would not remain as you are."

"But what can I do? Since I don't feel this same need, it could only come to me... well, from the outside. How else could it be?"

"You know you almost make me wish I was dead."

"Is it me in particular who has that effect, or were you just speaking in general?"

"Of course I was only speaking in general. In general about us both."

"Because there is another thing I would not really like, and that is to have provoked in anyone, even if only once, a feeling as violent as that."

"Oh, I'm sorry."

"It doesn't matter."

"And I would like to thank you too."

"But for what?"

"I don't really know. For your niceness."

II

T HE CHILD CAME OVER QUIETLY from the far side of the park and stood beside the girl.

"I'm thirsty," he announced.

The girl took a thermos and a mug from the bag beside her.

"I can well imagine," said the man, "that he must be thirsty after eating those sandwiches."

The girl opened the thermos. Still-warm milk steamed in the sunshine.

"But as you see," she said, "I have brought him some milk."

The child drank the milk greedily, then gave the mug back to the girl. A milky cloud stayed round his lips. The girl wiped them with a light and assured gesture. The man smiled at the child.

"If I said what I did," he remarked, "it was only to try and make myself clear. For no other reason."

Completely indifferent, the child contemplated this man who was smiling at him. Then he went back to the sandpit. The girl's eyes followed him.

"His name is Jacques," she said.

"Jacques," the man repeated.

But he was no longer thinking of the child.

"I don't know if you've noticed," he went on, "how traces of milk stay round children's mouths when they have drunk it? It's strange. In some ways they are so grown up: they seem to talk and walk like everyone else, and then when it comes to drinking milk, one realizes…"

"He doesn't say 'milk', he says 'my milk'."

"When I see something like that milk I suddenly feel full of hope, although I could never say why. As if some pain was deadened. I think perhaps that watching these children reminds me of the lions in those gardens. I see them as small lions, but lions all the same."

"Yet they don't seem to give you the same kind of happiness as those lions did in their cages facing the sun?"

"They give me a certain happiness, but you are right, not the same one. Somehow they always make you feel obscurely worried, and it is not that I particularly like lions: it would be untrue to say that. It was just a way of putting things."

"I wonder if you attach too much importance to that city, with the result that the rest of your life suffers by comparison? Or is it just that, never having been there,

I can hardly be expected to understand the happiness it gave you?"

"Perhaps, yes, it is probably to someone like you that I should most like to talk about it."

"Thank you. It was kind of you to say that. But you know I didn't want to imply that I was particularly unhappy – more unhappy, I mean, than anyone else would be in the same position. No, I was speaking of something quite different, something which I am afraid could not be solved by seeing any country, anywhere in the world."

"I'm sorry. You see, when I said that I should like to talk most about that country to someone like you, I did not mean for a second that you were unhappy without knowing it, and that telling you certain things would make you feel better. I simply meant that you seemed to me to be a person who might understand what I was trying to say better than most people. That's all, I assure you. But I expect I have talked too much about that city, and it is natural that you should have misunderstood."

"No, I don't think it is that. All I wanted was to put you right, in case you had made the mistake of thinking I was unhappy. Of course there are times when I cry, naturally there are, but it's only from impatience or irritation. I am not old enough yet to be profoundly sad about my life. That stage is yet to come."

"Yes, I really do see, but don't you think it is just possible that you might be wrong, and find no objection to it?"

"No, that would not be possible. Either I shall be unhappy in the same way as everyone else is, or I shall avoid being so to the best of my abilities. If life is terrible, I want to find out by myself, for my own sake, until the end and as completely as possible. And then I shall die as I mean to and someone will care. The only thing I ask for is a commonplace fate. But please tell me more of how you felt in that city."

"I am afraid I will tell it badly. I had no sleep and yet I was not tired, you understand?"

"And?…"

"I did not eat and I wasn't hungry."

"And then?…"

"All the minor problems of my life seemed to evaporate as if they had never existed except in my imagination. I thought of them as belonging to a distant past and laughed at them."

"But surely you must have wanted to eat and sleep in the end? It would have been impossible for you to go on without feeling tired or hungry."

"I expect so, but I didn't stay there long enough for those feelings to come back to me."

"And were you very tired when they did come back?"

"I slept for a whole day in a wood by the roadside."

"Like one of those scary tramps?"

"Yes, just like a tramp with my suitcase beside me."

"I understand."

"No, I don't think you can, yet."

"I mean, I am trying to understand, and one day I will. One day I shall understand what you have been saying to me completely. After all, anybody could, couldn't they?"

"Yes. I think one day you will understand them as completely as possible."

"Ah, if only you knew how difficult the things I was telling you about can be. How difficult it is to get for yourself, completely by yourself, just the things which are common to everyone. I mean above all how hard it is to fight the apathy which comes from wanting just the ordinary things which everyone else seems to have."

"I expect it is just that which prevents so many people from trying to achieve them. I admire you for trying to overcome these difficulties."

"Ah, if only willpower were enough! There have been men who found me attractive from time to time, but so far none of them has asked me to be his wife. There is a great difference between liking a young girl and wanting to marry her. And yet that must happen to me. Just once in my life I must be taken seriously. I wanted to ask you something: if you want a thing all the time, at every single moment of the day and night, do you think that you necessarily get it?"

"Not necessarily, no. But it still remains the best way of trying and the one with the greatest chance of success. I can really see no other way."

"After all, we're only talking. And as you don't know me or I you, you can tell me the truth."

"Yes, that's quite true, but really and truly I can see no other way. But perhaps I haven't had enough experience to answer your question properly."

"Because I once heard that quite the opposite was true: that it was by trying not to want something that it finally happened."

"But tell me, how could you manage not to want something when you want it so much?"

"That is exactly what I say to myself, and to tell you the truth I never felt that the other was a very serious idea. I think it must apply to people who want little things, to people who already have something and want something else, but not to people like us – sorry, I mean not to people like me who want everything, not just specifically but... I don't know how to say it..."

"In principle."

"Perhaps, yes. But please tell me more about your feelings for children. You said you were fond of them?"

"Yes. Sometimes, when I have no one else to talk to, I talk to them. But you know how it is: you can't really talk to children."

"Oh, you're right. We are the lowest of the low."

"But you mustn't think either that I am unhappy simply because sometimes I need to talk so badly that I talk to children. That's not true, because after all I must in some way have chosen my life or else I am just a madman indulging in his folly."

"I'm sorry. I didn't mean to say that. I simply saw the fine weather and the words came out of their own accord. You must try to understand me and not take umbrage, because sometimes fine weather makes me doubt everything – but it never lasts for more than a few seconds. I'm sorry."

"It doesn't matter. When I sit in garden squares like this, it is generally because I have been for some days without talking, when there have been no opportunities for conversation except with the people who buy my goods and they have been so rushed or standoffish that I could say nothing to them except the things that go with the sale of a reel of cotton. Naturally you mind this after some time, and suddenly you want to talk and be listened to so badly that it can even produce a feeling of illness like a slight fever."

"I know how you feel. You feel you could do without everything else, without eating, sleeping, anything rather than be silent. But in that city you were telling me about you didn't have to talk to children?"

"Not in that city, no. I was not with children then."

"That is what I thought."

"I used to see them in the distance. There were lots of them in the streets: they are left very free there, and from about the age of the one you look after, from about the age of five, they cross the whole town on their own to visit the zoo. They eat at any hour and sleep in the afternoon in the shadow of the lions' cages. Yes, I saw them in the distance sleeping in the shadow of those cages."

"It's true: children have all the time in the world, and they'll talk to anyone and always be ready to listen, but one hasn't very much to say to them."

"That's the trouble, yes: they don't have any prejudice against solitary people. In fact they like almost anyone, but then, as you said, there is so little to say to them."

"But tell me more."

"Oh, as far as children go, one person is as good as another, provided they talk about aeroplanes and trains. There is never any difficulty in talking to children about that sort of thing. It can become a little monotonous, but that's how it is."

"They can't understand other things – unhappiness for example – and I don't think it does much good to mention them."

"If you talk to them of things that don't interest them, they simply stop listening and wander off."

"Sometimes I have conversations on my own."

"That has happened to me too."

"I don't mean I talk to myself. I speak to a completely imaginary person, not just anybody, but to my worst enemy. You see, although I haven't any friends yet, I invent enemies."

"And what do you say to them?"

"I insult them, and always without the slightest explanation. Why do I do this, tell me?"

"Who knows? Probably because an enemy never understands you, and I think you would be hard put to it to accept being understood and to give in to the particular comfort it brings."

"After all, it's a form of talking isn't it? And it's unrelated to my work."

"Yes, it is talking, and since no one hears you and it gives you some satisfaction, it seems better to go on."

"When I spoke of the unhappiness which children cannot understand I was talking of unhappiness in general, the unhappiness everyone knows about, not of a particular kind of personal unhappiness."

"I understood that. The fact is we could not bear it if children could understand unhappiness. Perhaps they are the only people we cannot stand to see unhappy."

"There are not many happy people are there?"

"I don't think so. There are some who think it important to be happy and believe that they are, but deep down are not really as happy as all that."

"And yet I thought it was a duty for people to be happy, an instinct like going towards the sun rather than towards the darkness. Look at me for instance, at all the trouble I take over it."

"But of course it's like a duty. I believe that too. But if people feel the need for the sun it is because they know how sad the darkness can be. No one can live always in the darkness."

"I make my own darkness, but since other people seek the sun, I do so too, and that is what I feel about happiness. Everything I do is for my happiness."

"You are right, and that is probably why things are simpler for you than for other people: you have no alternative, while people who have a choice can long for things they know nothing about."

"You would think the gentleman where I am in service would be happy. He is a businessman with a great deal of money, and yet he always seems distracted, as if he were bored. I think sometimes that he has never looked at me, that he recognizes me without ever having seen me."

"And yet you are a person people would look at."

"But he doesn't see anyone. It is as if he no longer used his eyes. That is why he sometimes seems to me less happy than one might think. As if he were tired of everything, even of looking."

"And his wife?"

"His wife too. One could take her for being happy, but I know she is not."

"Don't you find that the wives of such men are easily frightened and have the tired, shaded look of women who no longer dream?"

"Not this one. She has a clear look and nothing catches her off her guard. Everyone thinks she has everything she could want, and yet I know it is not so. You learn about these things in my work. Often in the evening she comes into the kitchen with a vacant expression which doesn't deceive me, as if she wanted my company."

"It is just what we said: in the end people are not good at happiness. They want it of course, but when they have it they eat themselves away with dreaming."

"I don't know if it is that people are not good at happiness or if they don't understand what it is. Perhaps they don't really know what it is they want or how to make use of it when they have it. They may even get tired of trying to keep it. I really don't know. What I do know is that the word exists and that it was not invented for nothing. And just because I know that women, even those who appear to be happy, often start wondering towards evening why they are leading the lives they do, I am not going to start wondering if the word is meaningless. That is all I can say on the subject for now."

"Of course it is. And when I said that happiness is difficult to stand, I didn't mean that because of that it should be avoided. I wanted to ask you, is it around six o'clock when she comes into your kitchen? And does she ask you how you are getting on?"

"Yes, always around that time. I know what it means, believe me. I know it is a particular time of day when many women long for things they haven't got: but for all that I refuse to give up."

"It's always the same: when everything is there for things to go right people still manage to make them go wrong. They find happiness bitter."

"It makes no difference to me. I can only say again that I want to experience that particular sadness."

"If I said what I did, it was for no special reason. I was only talking."

"One could say that, without wanting to discourage me, you were, all the same, trying to warn me."

"Oh, hardly at all. Or only in the smallest degree, I promise you."

"But since my work has already shown me the other side of happiness, you need not worry. And in the end what does it matter if I find happiness or something else, as long as it is something real I can feel and deal with? Since I am in the world, I too must have my share of it. There is no reason why I should not. I will do just as everyone else does. You see I cannot imagine dying without having had the look that my employer has in her eyes when she comes to see me in the evening."

"It is hard to imagine you with tired eyes. You may not know it, but you have very fine eyes."

"They will be fine when they need to be."

"I can't help it, but the thought that one day you might have the same look as that woman is sad, that's all."

"Who can tell how things will turn out? And I will go through whatever is necessary. That is my greatest hope. And after my eyes have been fine they will become clouded like everyone else's."

"When I said that your eyes were fine, I meant that they had a wonderful expression."

"I am sure you are wrong, and even if you were right I couldn't be satisfied with it."

"I understand, and yet I find it hard not to tell you that for other people your eyes are very beautiful."

"Otherwise I would be lost. If for one moment I was satisfied with my eyes as they are, I would be lost."

"And so you were saying this woman comes into the kitchen?"

"Yes, sometimes. It is the only moment of the day when she does, and she always asks the same thing: how am I getting on?"

"As if things could go differently for you from one day to another?"

"Yes, as if they could."

"Such people have strange illusions about people like us. What else can you expect? And perhaps it is part of our job to preserve their illusions."

"Have you ever been dependent on a boss? It seems as if you must have, to understand so well."

"No. But it is a threat which hangs over people like us so constantly that it is easier to imagine than most things."

There was a fairly long silence between the girl and the man, and one would have thought them distracted, attentive only to the softness of the air. Then once again the man started to speak. He said:

"We really agree in principle, you know. You see, when I talked of this woman and of people who managed not to be entirely happy, I did not mean that it was a reason for not following their example, for not trying, in one's own turn and in one's own turn failing. Nor that one should deny longings such as you have for a gas stove, which would be to reject in advance all that might follow from it, such as a refrigerator or even happiness. I don't doubt the truth of your hopes for a moment. On the contrary, I think they are exactly what they should be. I really do."

"Must you go? Is that why you said all that?"

"No, I just didn't want you to misunderstand me, that's all."

"The way you talked like that, all of a sudden drawing conclusions from everything we had said, made me think that perhaps you had to go."

"No, I have no need to go. I just wanted to say that I completely agree with you. And I was going to add that if there was one thing I didn't quite understand – and I hate being a bore on this subject – it is still the fact that you take on so much extra work and that you always agree to do whatever they ask. Don't blame me for coming back to it, but I can't agree with you on this point, even if I do understand your reasons. I am afraid… what I am really afraid of is that you might feel that you must accept all the worst things that come your way in order to have earned the right one day to be finished with them for ever."

"And if that were the case?"

"Ah no. I cannot accept that. I don't believe that anything or anyone exists whose function it is to reward people for their personal merits, and certainly not people who are obscure or unknown. We are abandoned."

"But if I told you it was not for that reason, but so that I should never lose my horror for my work, so that I should go on feeling all the disgust I felt for it as much as ever?"

"I am sorry, but even then I could not agree. I think you have already begun to live your life, and even at the risk of repeating this endlessly to you and becoming a bore I really must say that I think things have already started for you, that time passes for you as much as for anyone else, and that even now you can waste it, lose it – as you do when you take on work which anyone else in your place would refuse."

"I think you must be very nice to be able to put yourself into other people's places and think for them with so much understanding. I could never do that."

"You have other things to do; I have the luxury, you see, of not having too much hope."

"Perhaps you're right. Perhaps the fact that I have decided to change everything is a sign that things have begun for me. And the fact that I cry from time to time is probably also a sign, and I expect I should no longer hide this from myself."

"Everyone cries, and not because of that, but simply because they are alive."

"But one day I checked with my trade union and I discovered that it was quite usual for maids to be expected to do most of the things I have to do. That was two years ago. For instance there's no reason why I shouldn't tell you that sometimes we have to look after very old women, as old as eighty-nine, weighing up to ninety-two kilos and no longer quite right in their minds, soiling their clothes at any hour of the day or night and whom nobody wants to bother about. It's such a struggle that, yes, I admit it, it sometimes leads to going all the way to the trade union. And it turns out that these things are not forbidden, that they haven't even been thought about. And even if they had been thought about, you know very well that you would always be able to find some among us who would be willing to do any kind of work, that there would always be people who would accept doing what we refuse to do, who could not avoid agreeing to do what everyone else would be too ashamed to do."

"Did you really say ninety-two kilos?"

"Yes, and last time she was weighed she had gained some. And yet, I would have you appreciate the fact that I haven't killed her, not even that time two years ago after I came back from the trade union. She was fat enough then and I was eighteen. I still haven't killed her and I never will, although it becomes easier and easier as she gets older and frailer. She is left alone in the bathroom to wash, and the bathroom is at the far end of the house. All I would have to do would be to hold her head under water for three minutes and it would be all over. She is so old that even her children wouldn't mind her death, nor would she herself, since she hardly knows she is there any more. But not only do I not do it, I look after her very well and always for the reasons I explained, because if I killed her it would mean that I could imagine improving my present situation, making it bearable. And if I took care of her badly, not only would that be contrary to my plan, but they would easily find someone else to do it better. 'Plenty more fish in the sea' – that's our only legal status. No, no one can rescue me except a man. I hope you don't mind my telling you all this."

"Ah, I no longer know what to say to you."

"Let's not talk about it any more."

"Yes, but still! You said it would be easy to get rid of that old woman and no one, not even she herself, would mind. Again, I am not giving you advice, let's be clear, but it seems to me that in many cases other people could do something of that nature to make their lives a little easier and still be able to hope for their future as much as before?"

"It's no good talking to me like that. I would rather my horror became worse. It is my only chance of getting out."

"After all, we were only talking. I just wondered whether it might not be almost a duty to prevent someone from hoping so much."

"There seems no reason why I shouldn't tell you that I know someone like me who tried, who did kill."

"I don't believe it. Perhaps she thought she had killed someone, but she couldn't really have done it."

"It was a dog. She was sixteen. You may say it is not at all the same thing as killing a person, but she did it and says it is very much the same."

"Perhaps she didn't give it enough to eat. That's not the same as killing."

"No, it was not like that. They both had exactly the same food. It was a very valuable dog and so they had the same food. Of course it was not the same as the things the people in the house ate, and she stole the dog's steak once. But that wasn't enough."

"She was young and longed for meat, as most children do."

"She poisoned the dog. She stayed awake a long time mixing poison with its food. She told me she didn't even think about the sleep she was losing. The dog took two days to die. Of course it is the same as killing a person. She knows. She saw it die."

"I think it would have been more unnatural if she had not done it."

"But why such hatred for a dog? In spite of all the food he ate, he was the only friend she had. One thinks one isn't nasty and yet, you see…"

"It is situations like that which should not be allowed. From the moment they arise the people involved cannot do otherwise than as they do. It is inevitable, quite inevitable."

"They found out she was the one who killed the dog. She got the sack. They could do nothing else to her, since it is not a crime to kill a dog. She said that she would almost have preferred them to punish her, she felt so guilty. Our work, you know, leads us to have the most terrible thoughts."

"Leave it then."

"I work all day and I would even like to work harder, but at something else: something in the open air which brings results you can see, which can be counted like other things, like money. I would rather break stones on the roads or work steel in a foundry."

"But do it then. Break stones on the road. Leave your present work."

"No, I can't. Alone, as I explained to you, alone I could not do it. I have tried, without success. Alone, without any affection, I think I should just die of hunger. I wouldn't have the strength to force myself to go on."

"There are women road-menders. I have seen them."

"I know. I think about them every day, you can be sure of that. But I should have started in that way. It's too late now. A job like mine makes you so disgusted with yourself that you have even less meaning outside it than in it. You don't even know that you exist enough for your own death to matter to you. No, from now on my only solution is a man, for whom I shall exist – only then will I get out."

"But do you know what that is called?"

"No. All I know is that I must persist in this slavery for some time longer before I can enjoy things again, things as simple as eating."

"Forgive me."

"It doesn't matter. I must stay where I am for as long as I have to. Please don't think that I lack goodwill, because it is not that. It is just that it is not worthwhile trying to make me hope less – as you put it – because if I tried to hope less than I do, I know that I would no longer hope at all. I am waiting. And while I wait I am careful not to kill anything, neither a person nor a dog, because those are serious things and could turn me into a nasty person for the rest of my life. But let's talk a little more about you: you who travel so much and are always alone."

"Well, yes, I travel and I am alone."

"Perhaps one day I will travel too."

"You can only see one thing at a time and the world is big, and you can only see it for yourself with your own two eyes. You can only see little of it, and yet most people travel."

"All the same, however little you can see, I expect it is a good way of passing the time."

"The best, I think, or at least it passes for the best. Being in a train absorbs time as much as sleeping. And a ship even more: you just look at the wakes following the ship and time passes by itself."

"And yet sometimes time takes so long to pass that you feel almost as if it were something which had been dragged out of your own insides."

"Why not take a little trip for eight days or so? For a holiday. You need only want to. Couldn't you do that? While still waiting of course?"

"It's true that waiting seems very long. I joined a political party, not because I thought it would make things move faster for me, but I thought it might make the time pass more quickly. But even so it is very long."

"But that is it exactly! Since you are already a member of a party, and you go to this dance hall, since in fact you are doing everything you can to be able to leave your present job one day, then surely you could also make a short journey while waiting for your life to take the turning you want it to?"

"I did not mean anything more than I said: that sometimes things seem very long."

"All you need to do is change your mood just a fraction, and then you could take a little voyage for eight days or so."

"On Saturday when I come back from dancing I cry sometimes, as I told you. How can you make a man desire you? Love cannot be forced. Perhaps it is the mood that you were talking about which makes me so undesirable: a feeling of rancour, and how could that please anyone?"

"I meant nothing more about your mood than that it prevented you from taking a holiday. I wouldn't advise you to become like me, a person who finds too much hope superfluous. But you must see that from the moment you decided it was best to let that old woman live out her days, and that you must do everything they ask of you, so as one day to be free to do something quite different, then it seems to me that as a kind of compensation you could take a short holiday and go away. Why, even I would do it."

"I understand, but tell me, what would I do with a holiday? I wouldn't know what to do with myself. I would simply be there looking at new things without them giving me any pleasure."

"You must learn, even if it is difficult. From now on, as a provision against the future, you must learn that. Looking at new things is something one learns."

"Yes, but tell me again, how could I ever manage to learn how to enjoy myself in the present when I am worn out with waiting for the future? I wouldn't have the patience to look at anything new."

"It doesn't matter. Forget about it. It wasn't very important."

"And yet if you only knew how much I would like to be able to look at new things."

"Tell me, when a man asks you to dance with him, do you immediately think he might marry you?"

"Yes. You see I'm too practical. All my troubles come from that. But how could I be anything else? It seems to me that I could never love anyone before I had some freedom, and that can only come to me through a man."

"And another question: if a man doesn't ask you to dance, do you still think he might marry you?"

"I don't think so much then, because I am at the dance hall. When I dance I get carried away by the movement and the excitement, and at those moments I think a man might most easily forget who I am, and even if he did find out he would mind it less under those circumstances than at any other time. I dance very well, and when I am dancing, my current position is not visible. I become like everyone else. I myself even forget who I am. Ah, sometimes I don't know what to do any more!"

"But do you think about it while you are at the dance hall?"

"No. There I think of nothing. I think before or afterwards. There it is as if I were asleep."

"Everything happens, believe me. We think that nothing will ever happen, but it does. There is not a man among all the millions who exist, not a single one, who hasn't known the things you are waiting for."

"I am afraid you don't really understand what it is I am waiting for."

"I am talking, you see, not only of the things you know you want, but also of the things you want without knowing. Of something less immediate, something of which you are still unaware."

"Yes, I follow what you are saying. And it is true that there are things I don't think of now. But all the same, I would so like to know how those things happen. Could you tell me, please?"

"They happen like anything else."

"Just as what I know I am waiting for?"

"Exactly. It is difficult to talk to you of things you know so little. I think that those things either come about suddenly, all at once, or else so slowly that you scarcely notice them. And when they have happened, when they are there, they don't seem at all surprising: it feels as if they had always been there. One day you will wake up and there it will all be. And it will be the same for the gas stove: you will wake up one day and not even be able to explain how it came to be there."

"But what about you? You who are always travelling and who seem, if I have understood you, to attach so little importance to events."

"But the same things can happen anywhere without any warning, in places like trains, and the only difference between the things which happen to me and those you want for yourself is that in my case they are without a future: there is nothing one can do with them."

"Oh, but it must be very sad to live as you do, always with events which can have no future! I think that from time to time you must cry too."

"But no, one gets used to it like everything else. And gracious me, everyone has cried at least once, every single one of all the millions of people on earth. That proves nothing in itself. Perhaps I should also explain that as far as I am concerned the tiniest thing can cheer me up. I like waking up in the morning, for instance, and quite often I find myself singing while I shave."

"Oh, but surely singing proves nothing, as you would put it yourself?"

"But you must understand, I like being alive, and I should have thought that was the one point on which no one could make a mistake."

"I don't know what it feels like. Perhaps that is why I understand you so badly."

"Whatever the cause of your unhappiness – and I really can find no other word for it – you must, you really must, show a little goodwill."

"But I am worn out with waiting and yet I go on waiting. It is more than I can do to wash that old woman, and yet I go on washing her. I do all the things which are really too much for me. What more do you ask?"

"By goodwill I mean that you could, perhaps, wash her as you would wash anything else – a saucepan for example."

"No, I tried that, but it was no good. She smiles, she smells bad. She is human."

"Alas. What can you do?"

"Sometimes I don't know myself. I was sixteen when this life began for me. At the beginning I didn't pay much attention, and now look where I am. I am twenty and nothing has happened to me, nothing, and that old woman never manages to die and is still there. And nobody has asked me to be his wife. Sometimes I even think I must be dreaming, that somehow I must be inventing so many difficulties."

"Why not work for another family? One where there are no old people? Find a place with some advantages – although naturally I know they could only be relative."

"No, they would always treat me as something apart. In my kind of work changing jobs means nothing, since the only real change would be for such jobs to be abolished. If I did manage to find a family such as you describe, I wouldn't really be able to put up with them any better than I do with my present one. And then just through changing and changing, without really changing anything, I would end by believing in – I hardly know what – some sort of fate, and that would be worse than anything. No, I must stay where I am right up to the moment when I can leave for ever. Sometimes I believe in it so much. I can hardly tell you how much. As much as I know I am sitting here."

"Well, then, while staying where you are, you could still take that little journey. I believe you could."

"Yes, perhaps. Perhaps I could make that journey."

"Of course you could."

"But, from all you said, that city you talked about must be very far away. Immensely far."

"I reached it by little stages, taking fifteen days in all, stopping off here and there for a day at a time. But someone who could afford to do so could reach it in one night on the train."

"You can be there in a night?"

"Yes, and already it is full summer there. Of course I couldn't be certain that someone else would find it as beautiful as I did. I suppose it is quite possible that someone else might not like it at all. I imagine I didn't see it with the same eyes as a person who found nothing there but the place itself."

"But if one knew in advance that another person had been happy there, I think one would look at it with different eyes. We're only talking, aren't we?"

"Yes."

They were silent. Imperceptibly the sun was sinking ,and once more a memory of winter lay over the city. It was the girl who started the conversation again.

"What I meant," she began, "was that something of that happiness must remain in the air. Don't you agree?"

"I don't know."

"I would like to ask you something more. Could you tell me more about those things we were discussing – the things that could take place in a train for example?"

"Not really. They happen, that's all. You know, few people would put up with a commercial traveller of my status."

"But I am only a maid and I still hope. You mustn't talk like that."

"I am sorry. I explained myself badly. You will change, but I don't think I will, or rather I don't think so any more. And whichever way you look at it, there is nothing to be done about it. Even if I could have wished that things had been different, I can never forget the commercial traveller I have become. When I was twenty I wore white shorts and played tennis. That is how my life started. I mean a life can begin anyhow – a fact we do not appreciate enough. And then time passes and we discover that life has very few solutions; and things become established until one fine day we find they are so established that the very idea of changing them seems absurd."

"That must be a terrible moment."

"No. It passes unnoticed as time passes. But you mustn't be sad. I am not complaining about my life, and to tell you the truth I don't think about it much. The least thing amuses me."

"And yet you give the impression of not having told the whole truth about your life."

"I assure you I am not someone to be pitied."

"I too know that life is terrible. I am not as stupid as that. I know it is as terrible as it is good."

Once more silence fell between the man and the girl. The sun was sinking even lower.

"Although I only took the train in small stages," the man said, "I don't think it can be very expensive."

"I spend very little money," said the girl. "In fact the only expenses I have are connected with dancing. So you see, even if the train was expensive I could still afford the journey if I wanted to. But I am afraid that wherever I was I would feel I was wasting my time. I would say to myself: what are you doing here instead of being at that dance hall? For the moment your place is there and nowhere else. Wherever I was I would think of it.

If it interests you, the dance hall is in the fourteenth. A lot of soldiers go there and unfortunately they never think of marrying, but there are other people too and one never knows. Yes, it's on Rue de la Croix-Nivert, and it's called the Croix-Nivert Dance Hall."

"Thank you. But you know they also have dances in that city, and if you did decide to make the journey you could go to them. And no one would know who you were there."

"Are they held in the gardens?"

"Yes, in the open air. On Saturdays they last all night."

"I see. But then I would have to lie about what I am. I know you will say that it's not my fault that I have to do the job I do, but it still makes me feel as if I had a crime to conceal."

"But since you want to change so much, surely concealing it would only be a half-lie?"

"I think I could only lie about something for which I was responsible, but not about anything else. And although it sounds strange, I feel almost as if I had chosen that particular dance hall and that what I want must happen there. It's a small one, but it suits me as I really have no illusions about what I am or what I might become. I would feel strange and out of place anywhere else. If you were to come there we could have a dance or two while waiting for someone else to ask me. I mean if you would like to, of course. I dance well and I've never been taught."

"I dance well too."

"Don't you find that strange? Why should we dance well? Why us rather than anyone else?"

"Us rather than the people who dance badly you mean?"

"Yes, I know some. If you could only see them. They have no idea at all. It's double Dutch to them…"

"But you're laughing."

"What else can I do? People who dance badly always make me laugh. They try, they concentrate and there's nothing to be done about it: they simply can't manage."

"It must be because dancing is something which cannot entirely be learnt, you know. Do the ones you know hop or shuffle?"

"She hops and he shuffles with the result… I can hardly describe it to you. And yet it's obviously not their fault."

"No, it's not their fault. And yet it's difficult not to feel that somehow there is a certain justice in the fact that they can't dance."

"We may be wrong."

"Yes, we may be, and after all it doesn't matter so much whether one dances well or badly."

"No, it's of no great importance. Yet all the same it's as if we had a secret strength concealed in us. Oh, nothing very much of course... And yet don't you think I'm right?"

"But they could just as easily have been good dancers."

"Yes, that's true, but then there would be something else, although I can't imagine what, which we would have and they would not: I don't know what it would be, but it would be something."

"I don't know either, but I think you're right."

"I must admit, I love dancing. It is probably the only thing I do now which I would like to go on doing for the rest of my life."

"I feel the same. I think everyone likes dancing, even people like us, and perhaps we would not be such good dancers if we didn't enjoy it so much."

"But perhaps we don't know exactly how much we do enjoy it? How could we know?"

"I don't think it matters. If it suits us so well we should go on not knowing."

"But the dreadful part is that when the dance is over I start remembering. It's Monday and I mutter 'old bitch' as I wash her. I don't think I'm a nasty person, but of course I have no one to reassure me on this point and so I can only believe myself. When I say 'bitch', she smiles."

"I can tell you that you are not a nasty person."

"But when I think about them my thoughts are so evil, if you only knew, just as if it was all their fault. I try to reason with myself, but I can never manage to think in any other way."

"Don't worry about those thoughts. You are not a nasty person."

"Do you really think so?"

"I do. One day you will be very giving, with yourself and with your time."

"You really are nice."

"But I didn't say that out of niceness."

"But you, what will happen to you?"

"Nothing. As you can see, I am no longer very young."

"But you, you who once thought of killing yourself – because you did say that."

"Oh that was only laziness at the thought of having to go on feeding myself: nothing serious really."

"But that's impossible. Something will happen to you or else it will only be because you don't want anything to happen."

"Nothing happens to me except the things that happen to everyone, every day."

"You say that, but in that city?"

"There I was not alone. And then, afterwards, I was alone again. I think it was just luck."

"No. When someone is without any hope at all, as you are, it is because something happened to him: it's the only explanation."

"One day you will understand. There are people like me, people who get so much pleasure from just being alive that they can get by without hope. I sing while I shave – what more do you want?"

"But were you unhappy after you left that city?"

"Yes."

"And did you think of staying in your room and never leaving it again?"

"No, not then. Because then I knew that it is possible not to be alone, even if only by accident."

"Tell me what else you do, after the morning."

"I sell my goods, then I eat, then I travel, then I read the newspapers. I can't tell you how much I enjoy the newspapers. I read them from cover to cover, including the advertisements. I get so absorbed in a newspaper that when I put it down I have to think for a minute who I am."

"But I meant other things: what do you do apart from all the obvious things, apart from shaving and selling your goods and taking trains and eating and reading the newspapers? I mean those things which no one appears to be doing, but which everyone is doing all the same."

"I see what you mean… But I really don't know what I do apart from the things I mentioned. I don't deny that sometimes I do wonder what I am doing, but just wondering doesn't seem to be enough. I probably don't wonder hard enough, and I think it's perfectly possible that I shall never know. You see, I believe that it is quite usual to be like me, and that a great many people go through life without ever exactly knowing why."

"But it seems to me that one could try to know a little harder than you do."

"But I hang by a thread. I even hold on to myself by the merest thread. So you see, life is easier for me than it is for you, which explains everything. And then too I can manage to live without having to know certain things."

Once more they were silent. Then the girl went on:

"I still can't understand. Forgive me for going back to the subject, but I still can't understand how you came to be as you are, nor even how you came to do the lowly job you do."

"As I told you: little by little. My brothers and sisters are all successful people who knew what they wanted.

As for me, once again, I didn't know. They can't understand either how I managed to come down so much in the world."

"That seems an odd way of putting it: I would say 'become discouraged' would be more accurate. And it's still beyond me to understand how you ended up where you are."

"Perhaps it comes from the fact that the idea of success was always a little vague in my mind. I never quite understood what it had to do with me. And, after all, I don't find my work quite so lowly."

"I am sorry to have used that expression, although I thought it would have been all right coming from me, since my own work can hardly even be described as work. I only said that to try and make you tell me more. I wanted you to see that I found you mysterious, not that I was blaming you."

"I understood that, and I'm sorry I took you up on that term. I know there are people in the world who can judge what I do on its own merits and not necessarily despise it. I didn't mind anything you said. To tell you the truth I was only half aware of what I was saying myself. I am afraid it always bores me to talk of my own past."

Again they were silent. This time the memory of winter became insistent. The sun would no longer reappear: it had reached the stage where it was hidden by the mass of the city's buildings. The girl remained silent. The man started to talk to her again:

"I wanted to say," he went on, "that I would be very unhappy if you thought, even for an instant, that I was trying to influence you in any way. Even when we talked about that old woman we were, after all, only talking…"

"Please, let's not talk about that any more."

"No, let's not talk about it. I was just trying to tell you that by dint of understanding people, or at least trying to put yourself in their shoes, to look for what can relieve them of waiting for so long, you make certain assumptions and hypotheses – but from that position to that of giving advice there is an enormous step, and I would feel cross with myself for having overstepped that boundary without knowing it…"

"Please, let's not talk about me any more."

"All right."

"But I wanted to ask you something. What happened after you left that city?…"

The man was silent, and the girl did not try to break his silence. Then, when she no longer seemed to expect a reply, he said:

"I told you. After that city, I was unhappy."

"But how unhappy?"

"I believe as unhappy as it is possible to be. I thought I had never been unhappy before."

"Did that feeling go eventually?"

"Yes, in the end."

"You were never alone in that city?"

"Never."

"Neither during the day nor the night?"

"Never, not by day nor by night. It lasted eight days."

"And then you were alone again. Completely alone?"

"Yes. And I have been alone ever since."

"I suppose it was tiredness that made you sleep all day with your suitcase beside you?"

"No, it was unhappiness."

"Yes, you did say you were as unhappy as it was possible to be. Do you still believe that?"

"Yes."

It was the girl's turn to be silent.

"Please don't cry, I beg you," the man said, smiling.

"I can't help myself."

"Things happen like that. Things that cannot be avoided, that no one can avoid."

"Oh, it is not that. Those things hold no terrors for me."

"And you want them too."

"Yes, I want them."

"You are right, because nothing is so worth living through as the things which make one so unhappy. Don't cry."

"I'm not crying any more."

"You will see. Before the summer is out you will open that door and it will be for ever."

"Sometimes it almost doesn't seem to matter any more."

"But you will see. You will see. It will happen quite quickly."

"It seems to me you should have stayed in that town. You should have tried to stay by all possible means."

"I stayed as long as I could."

"No, I don't believe you did everything. I cannot believe it."

"I did everything I thought could be done. Perhaps I didn't go about it in the right way. Don't think about it any more. You will see: before the summer is out things will have turned out all right for you."

"Perhaps. Who knows? Sometimes I wonder if it is all worth so much trouble."

"Of course it is. And after all, as you said yourself, since we are here – we didn't ask to be, but here we are – we must take the trouble. There is nothing else we can do, and you will do it. Before the summer is out you will have opened that door."

"Sometimes I think I will never do it. That when I am ready to open it I will draw back."

"No. You will open it."

"If you say that, it must be because you think I have chosen the best way of getting what I want, of ending my present life and finally becoming something?"

"Yes, I do think so. I think the way you have chosen is the best for you."

"If you say that, it must be because you think there are other ways which other people would have taken."

"I expect there are other ways, but I also believe they would suit you less well."

"Are you sure of what you are saying?"

"I believe what I am saying, but neither I nor anyone else could tell you with complete certainty."

"I ask because you said you understood things through travelling and seeing so many different places and people."

"Perhaps I understand less well where hope is concerned. I think that if I understand anything it's probably more the small, ordinary things of everyday life: little problems rather than big ones. And yet I can say this: even if I am not absolutely and entirely sure of the means you have chosen, I am absolutely and entirely sure that before this summer is out you will have opened that door."

"Thank you all the same, very much. But tell me once again, what about you?"

"Spring is on its way, and with it the fine weather. I will be off again."

They were silent one last time. And one last time it was the girl who took up the conversation:

"What was it that made you get up and start off again after sleeping in the wood?"

"I don't really know. It probably just had to be done."

"A short while ago you said it was because from then on you knew it was possible not to be alone, even if only by accident."

"No, it was later that I knew that. Some days later. At the time it was different. I knew nothing at all."

"You see how different we really are. I think I should have refused to get up."

"But of course you would not. What or whom would you have refused?"

"Nothing or no one. I would have simply refused."

"You're wrong. You would have done as I did. It was cold, I was cold, and I got up."

"But we are different all the same."

"Oh, doubtless we are different in the way we take our troubles."

"No, I think we are even more different than that."

"I don't think so. I don't think we are more different than anyone is different from anyone else."

"Perhaps I am mistaken."

"Since we understand each other? Or at least we try to. And we both like dancing. You said you went to the Croix-Nivert?"

"Yes. It is a well-known place. A lot of people like us go there."

III

T HE CHILD CAME OVER QUIETLY from the far side of the garden square and stood beside the girl.

"I'm tired," he announced.

The man and the girl looked around them. It was darker than it had been. It was evening.

"It is late, for sure," said the girl.

This time the man made no comment. The girl wiped the child's hands, picked up his toys and put them into her bag, all without rising from the bench. Tired of playing, the child sat down at her feet to wait.

"Time seems shorter when one is talking," said the girl.

"And then afterwards, suddenly, much longer."

"Yes, like another kind of time. But it does one good to talk."

"Yes it does one good. It is only afterwards that it is rather sad: after one has stopped talking. Then time becomes too slow. Perhaps one should never talk."

"Perhaps," said the girl after a pause.

"Only because of the slowness afterwards: that was all I meant."

"And perhaps because of the silence to which we are both returning."

"Yes, it is true that we are both returning to silence. It seems as though we are already there."

"No one will talk to me again this evening: I will go to bed in silence. And I am only twenty. What have I done to the world that my life should be like this?"

"Nothing. There are no answers to be found in thinking in that direction. You should be thinking rather of what you will do to the world. Yes, perhaps one should never talk. When one starts it is like picking up a delightful habit one had abandoned, even if it is a habit one had never quite acquired."

"Yes, that is right. As if we knew how wonderful it was to talk. It must be a very deep instinct to be so strong."

"And to be talked to is as deep and as natural an instinct."

"I expect so, yes."

"Later you will understand how much. At least for your sake I hope that you will."

"I have talked so much that I feel ashamed."

"Oh, that is the very last thing you should worry about, if indeed there is any need for you to worry at all."

"Thank you."

The girl rose from the bench. The child got up and took her hand. The man remained seated.

"It is getting quite cold," the girl said.

"Yes, it is not yet summer, although sometimes, during the day, one has the illusion that it is already here."

"Yes, one forgets, it's true. It is rather like going back into silence after talking."

"Yes, it is the same thing."

The child tugged at the girl's hand.

"I'm tired," he repeated.

The girl did not seem to have heard the child.

"I really must go back," she said at last.

The man made no move. His eyes rested vaguely on the child.

"And you, are you not leaving?" asked the girl.

"No. I will stay here until the square closes and go then."

"Have you nothing to do this evening?"

"No. Nothing in particular."

"I must go back," said the girl after a moment's hesitation.

The man rose slightly from the bench, and very lightly blushed.

"Could you not – just for once, I mean – go back a little later?"

For a space the girl hesitated, and then she pointed at the child:

"I wish I could, but I cannot."

"I only meant that it seems to me that it does you good to talk. Particularly you. That was all I meant."

"Oh, I understood that, but I cannot stay. I am late already."

"Well then, I must say goodbye. You said it was on Saturdays that you went to the Croix-Nivert dance hall?"

"Yes. Every Saturday. If you came there we could have a dance together. If you would like to, I mean."

"Yes, perhaps we could. If you would allow me to invite you?"

"I simply meant for the fun of it."

"That is how I understood you. Well, perhaps we shall meet again. On Saturday perhaps – one never knows."

"Perhaps. Well, goodbye."

"Goodbye."

The girl took two steps and then turned back:

"I wanted to say… all I wanted to say was, why don't you go for a walk… instead of sitting there waiting for the square to close."

"It is kind of you, but I think I would prefer to remain here until it shuts."

"But just a little walk, for no particular reason. Just to look at things."

"No, thank you. I really prefer to remain here. A walk doesn't appeal to me."

"It is going to become colder… and if I am so insistent it is only because… because perhaps you do not know what garden squares are like towards closing time, how sad they can be…"

"I do know. But I would rather stay here."

"Do you always do that? Always wait for squares to close?"

"No. Generally I am like you: it is a moment I avoid. But today I want to wait for it."

"Perhaps you have your own reasons," said the girl reflectively.

"I am a coward, that is why."

The girl moved back a step towards him.

"Oh, if you say that," she said, "it must be because of me, because of what I said."

"No. It is because somehow this time of day always makes me want to recognize and to speak the truth."

"Please don't say things like that."

"But surely my cowardice was clear in every word I said, ever since we started talking."

"No. It is not the same thing as saying it all at once, in one word. You are wrong."

The man smiled.

"Believe me, it is not such a very serious matter."

"But I cannot understand why the fact that a square is closing should suddenly make you discover that you are a coward."

"Because I do nothing to avoid... despair. On the contrary."

"But in that case what difference could a walk make?"

"To do anything to avoid it would be courageous. To create any diversion, however small."

"I beg of you. Just take a little walk."

"No. It would not be possible. My whole life is like this."

"But try just once! Try."

"No, I don't want to start to change."

"Ah! I see that I have talked far too much."

"On the contrary. It was the great pleasure had in listening to you that made me understand so well what I am really like: how submerged in cowardice. It is not your fault: I am no worse than I was yesterday, for example, and no better."

"I am afraid I do not understand cowardice very well, but I know that yours suddenly seems to make my courage a little despicable."

"And to me, you see, your courage makes my cowardice appear more dreadful still. That is what it means to talk."

"It is as if, after knowing you, courage became slightly useless, a thing which, finally, one could do without."

"In the end we only do what we can, you with your courage and me with my cowardice, and that is all that matters."

"You are probably right, but why is it that courage seems so unattractive and cowardice so appealing? For it is like that isn't it?"

"It is all cowardice. If you only knew how easy it was."

The little boy pulled at the girl's hand.

"I'm tired," he said again.

The man raised his eyes and seemed troubled.

"Do you think I am wrong?"

"Inevitably."

"I am sorry."

"Ah, if only you knew how little it mattered. It is as if someone other than I were involved."

They waited a few moments in silence. The square was emptying. At the ends of the streets the sky showed pink.

"It is true," the girl said finally, and her voice was almost the voice of sleep, "that we do what we can, you with your cowardice and I with my courage."

"And yet we manage to earn our living. We have at least managed that."

"Yes, that is true: we have managed that as well as anyone else."

"And from time to time we even manage to talk."

"Yes, even if it makes us unhappy afterwards."

"Everything, no matter what, makes one unhappy. Sometimes even eating."

"You mean eating after one has been hungry for too long?"

"Yes, just that."

The child started to whimper. The girl looked at him as though for the first time.

"I do have to go," she said.

She turned again to the child.

"Just for once," she said to it gently, "just for once you must be good."

And she turned again to the man.

"And so I will say goodbye."

"Goodbye. Perhaps we will meet again at the dance hall."

"Perhaps. You do not know yet if you will go there?"

The man made an effort to reply.

"Not yet, no."

"How strange that is."

"If you only knew what a coward I am."

"But you mustn't let going to the dance hall depend on your cowardice."

The man made a further effort to reply.

"It is very difficult for me to know yet whether I will go. I cannot, no I cannot know now whether I will or not."

"But you do go dancing from time to time?"

"Yes, without knowing anyone."

It was the girl's turn to smile.

"But just for the fun of it, that is all you must think of. And you will see how well I dance."

"Believe me, if I went it would be for fun."

The girl smiled even more. But it was a smile the man could ill support.

"I thought, if I understood you correctly, that you reproached me for allowing too little place for pleasure in my life?"

"It was true, yes."

"You said I should be less suspicious of it than I am."

"You know so little about it, if you only knew how little!"

"You must excuse me for saying this, but I have the feeling that perhaps you know less about it than you imagine. I was talking of the pleasure of dancing of course."

"Yes, of dancing with you."

The child started whimpering again.

"We are going," the girl said to him, and to the man: "I must say goodbye. Perhaps then we shall meet again this coming Saturday?"

"Perhaps, yes, perhaps. Goodbye."

The girl turned and went off rapidly with the child. The man watched her going, watched her as long as he could. She did not turn back.

CALDER PUBLICATIONS
EDGY TITLES FROM A LEGENDARY LIST

Changing Track
Michel Butor

Moderato Cantabile
Marguerite Duras

Jealousy
Alain Robbe-Grillet

The Blind Owl and Other Stories
Sadeq Hedayat

Locus Solus
Raymond Roussel

Cain's Book
Alexander Trocchi

Young Adam
Alexander Trocchi

CALDER

www.calderpublications.com